# PROFOUNI
# FROM THE COW TANK

## A Collection of Fifteen Short Stories

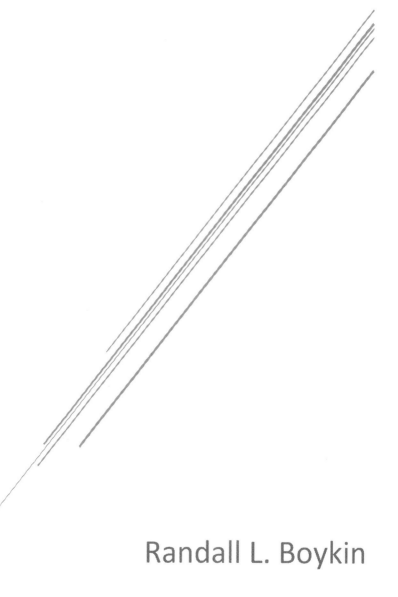

Randall L. Boykin

**For Robin.**

# Preface

Life... is... short.

You never know how much time you have in this life. Today you're here, tomorrow, who knows. You must embrace whatever life you are given.

For instance, growing up in a small town, me and my siblings begged for a swimming pool. Being that our parents were Teachers, we knew we couldn't afford one. Just the price of installing, much less maintaining a pool is more money than our parent's annual salary. So, being as resourceful, creative, and frugal as possible, my Dad went down to Osborne's Farm and Ranch supply and bought a cow tank.

Oh yes, there is nothing quite like a water stock/cow tank converted into a poor man's swimming pool. The more people I told, the more I discovered that some of my friends had similar versions of a swimming pool. Ironically, I guess it's true that ingenuity is the Mother of Invention.

I would never want to replace the memories of my Dad associated with that cow tank. I still chuckle thinking about all of it. Some things I took for granted regarding the entire memory:

Drinking from a water hose

The process of adding water to our swimming pool/cow tank from that same water hose

Vapors rising off the water from that sizzling, metal, cow tank (which had sat in 100 plus degree heat all day)

A yard of dead, yellowed grass, except for a bright green circle surrounding our pool

And the word Tepid... that's the word my Dad would describe the water as he got into our pool.

And like I stated previously, life is short. I do try to embrace whatever moment I am experiencing. However, looking back on the year 2001, my attitude and life seemed very different, and very bleak.   In the twenty plus years, I have learned that time does heal wounds... but you must give time... time.

So, here is some profound wisdom from my cow tank:

"Time heals wounds, but you will always have a scar."

"Everybody has a snake, and everybody has a snake-bite."

"Use it up, wear it out, make it do, or do without."

"Not my pasture, not my BS."

"It is... what it is."

So, here are some stories that just might be, might have been, thought of, or told, in my own 'cow tank'. Hope you enjoy them as much as I have enjoyed them.

Thanks for reading,

Randy... of course.

# Table of Content

# LEMON BARS

The new Reverend already had connections with many of his Parishioners. Many years ago, his late Grandfather had been a Minister at this very Church. So, when he was appointed the new Preacher at this small-town Congregation, he was elated with excitement. He never had a second thought until he was approached by Mrs. Alexander. It had only been two weeks since he agreed to judge the dessert contest for the Thanksgiving Carnival. He quickly realized he might have bitten off more than he could chew... figuratively, and literally.

Before he could thank Mrs. Alexander for volunteering to be the Chair of the Carnival, Mrs. Alexander reintroduced herself. With an authoritative tone she stated: "I prefer being addressed as Mrs. Anne Elizabeth Alexander". Continuing with her own form of Aristocracy, she informed the 'Reverend Jackson' that she and her late husband owned the largest land holdings within the neighboring eleven counties, and her late Father, who founded the Elizabeth Bank, kept EVERYONE afloat during the Great Depression. She, herself was an Entrepreneur in her own right, and owned many of the businesses within 'our small community'. Being 'Mrs. Anne Elizabeth Alexander' held great responsibility. She concluded with a 'he should have known' air that she takes these responsibilities quite seriously.

Suddenly, Reverend Jackson was more than a little concerned regarding future dealings with 'Mrs. Anne Elizabeth Alexander'. But all anxiety quickly faded when he discovered she was a master planner. Everything, absolutely everything was coordinated, executed, and delivered with perfection. The

Reverend was quite impressed. It seemed the more he complimented her, the happier she seemed to become.

The young Reverend's excitement continued to build. Participating in such a fun, family atmosphere at his new Parsonage, was like one of his dreams coming true. And now, it was Thanksgiving Carnival time.

One by one, the ladies of the Community Church, lined up to list their pies and cakes.

Just before the contest was to begin, Mrs. Alexander approached the table with a two-tiered cookie tower, covered in tiny lemon squares. She had cut her lemon bars into fourths and small enough so that everyone could taste some of her "delectable sweets". That's when he knew he was doomed.

Mrs. Eulalia Coffee had brought her Lemon Bars too. Everyone knew about and looked forward to her Lemon Bars. She was a Town Legend. Mrs. Coffee had won 'Grand Prize' for fourteen consecutive years. That's when Mrs. Alexander told Mrs. Coffee to brace herself this year. This year was her year to win. Mrs. Coffee replied kindly by saying, "I really hope you do."

There was no time like the present to begin the judging. Reverend Jackson's stomach was churning with nervousness. He could feel the ladies' eyes were watching him.

Using a tiny steno-pad, he would jot short notes about each dessert. The young Reverend moved forward and continued tasting each of the desserts. The process seemed to take forever. It was finally time for him to read off his winning selections.

The Reverend walked up the tiny stage to make his presentations. Voice cracking, he announced category by category, ending with The Grand Prize. Holding up the tiny gold plastic trophy, he announced the winner.

"Mrs. Anne Elizabeth Alexander!"

The entire audience gasped with utter shock.

Mrs. Alexander rushed up the rickety stage to retrieve her trophy. She acted as though she had just won an Academy Award. Without a moment hesitation, she proceeded with a prepared acceptance speech. She purposefully mispronounced yet thanked "Miss Eula" for her stiff competition. She ended with a trite "better luck next year".

As the evening finally closed, all the bakers began retrieving their plates. Like everyone else, Mrs. Coffee walked over to get her plate. Not one crumb was left of her Lemon Bars. Turning toward the Reverend, Mrs. Coffee apologized by saying "I'm so sorry. I forgot to hold one back for you." She glanced back to the two-tiered tower, still mostly full of soggy Lemon Cubes. Subtly she leaned and whispered "Today, you made your Grandad really proud."

Reverend Jackson replied, "Thanks Nana. I love you too."

# FAT GIRL

Bent over to stretch, Bryan crossed one leg over the other, then repeated the process for the other leg. Then he lunged forward, and then sideways. He even stretched his torso and arms toward the sky. Bryan was making sure he was properly loosened up before he began his run. Today of all days, he needed this run. He was still angry from yesterday.

Thinking to himself, 'How could she... and on Christmas Eve.'

He couldn't stop thinking about his Sister's words.

'Words matter, and she knows it. Words hurt... and can wound deeper than any cuts... or scrapes... AND with lasting effects. She should have known better. Actually, she KNOWS better... after all, she has a freaking Master's in PSYCHOLOGY!'

His sister Gigi was always reviving some childhood trauma. Every year was something different from their past. She would make declarations, that everything, and all of her rage was the family's fault. Most of their lives, their Father had been verbally and physically abusive. It wasn't just to her; it was to all of them. But for the past twenty years, every Holiday, every Birthday celebration, and every, single occasion, everyone walked on eggshells around her. She had replaced their Father's fury with her own anger and resentment. Unfortunately, she decided to use this particular Holiday to attack Bryan's daughter.

Bryan stopped stretching and started running. As he began to run, he started analyzing everything from the prior day, and their complicated past.

Usually, Gigi's blunt, verbal abuse was only heaped upon the adults. But this Christmas Eve, when she directed her anger toward everyone including the children, this was Bryan's turning point. This was his last straw. But he had guilt, too.


'I should have never formed a fist. I know Ava saw me do it. I know... and Ava knows... she knows I don't condone violence...'

As he began to develop a rhythm, his breathing steadied. He kept thinking 'I preach, and I preach that violence never solves anything, and yet I... her own Dad formed a fist... DANGIT! I let her down.'

The run felt good. Running helped him get control of his mind and emotions. It felt great to create a different rhythm. Running had become his therapy during college. He knew why he was running today. He kept hoping that this run would create the endorphins to develop some therapeutic response and take care of what was bothering him.

Running alone allowed him to sort through everything. Running had always helped him in the past. Maybe he could find some solution without fracturing his family. His reaction to Gigi was reprehensible.

'I should have never yelled back... especially in front of the kids. I should have responded differently... calmly... like she was a child... like... she was my child... taking her to another room... making her sit on the bed... reflecting on her behavior...'

Now huffing and puffing, he could feel himself pounding the pavement harder. The more he thought about her behavior, the angrier he became. He just wanted to run... and run hard. His laser focus was feeling his feet hit the road, ignoring the rest of the world.

'I should have never made a fist. I should have never made a fist.'

'And she saw me. Ava SAW me. I will not be like him. I will not be like him! I am not like him... I should have never made that fist.'

He started running faster. He ran faster and harder toward something that didn't exist. He was running for escape; for freedom; from his memory, from his Father, from his Sister; from his shame, and from his guilt. He was running from everything that he knew needed to happen. He was running toward a resolution he couldn't find.

....................................................................................................

After twenty minutes, Bryan suddenly saw he was on the backside of the lake.

Out loud, Bryan said, "What's the difference between a Lake and a Reservoir?" Breathing heavily, he stopped for a moment. He bent over, looking up and around trying to catch his breath. The distraction from a different thought, and catching his breath momentarily calmed him down.

He started running again, but this time at a slower pace. Instantly, he decided to go ahead and run the remainder of the lake. Today, he had the energy. It might be energy from anger, but he had the energy to finish it.

....................................................................................................

Finally emerging from the wooded area at the end of the regular trail, he knew he was only a couple of minutes from his car. By now, cold sweat was dripping down his head, down his neck and soaking his back. He was now approaching his old Honda which was sitting alone in the parking lot.

As he finally stopped in front of his car, he began stretching once again. He wasn't 20 years old anymore, and knew he needed to stretch. His muscles needed to calm down after the extra exertion.

As he stretched, he thought to himself, 'I've run this entire lake, and haven't solved anything. What am I going to do about her?'

But then, he had a revelation. Thinking out loud, he said "Wait... I'm not Dad... She is." This revelation, which slowly developed half-way around the lake, was the actual lightbulb moment he needed.

....................................................................................................

After Bryan got home, he went directly inside. He showered, got dressed and came back out to join the family. Most of his family were still sitting around the living room talking. His wife Maddie looked at him and asked, "Are you ok?"

"I am. I'm actually great! Now." Then turning toward his sister he said, "Gigi, we need to talk. Come with me, please."

"I'm BUSY!"

Bryan almost yelled saying, "NOW", and walked out of the Living Room.

Rolling her eyes, and getting out of one of the recliners, Gigi followed Bryan down the hall. They both entered the Master bedroom, just off the main hallway. He asked her to have a seat pointing at the corner of their bed. Gigi refused while nodding her head to her to the left, looking back and yelling "WHAT!" Then, with an exasperated tone, "WELL... what do you want?"

Calmly Bryan said, "Ok. Have it your way. You will go to the room you're staying, get your things packed and leave. You are no longer welcome in my house. Actually, you are no longer welcome in my HOME."

Gigi started screaming at him. Bryan just turned and walked out of the bedroom. Outside the doorway in the hall stood Maddie who made eye contact with Bryan as he was leaving the room. Suddenly Gigi yelled, "DON'T HIT ME AGAIN!" Bryan stopped, turned back, looked at Gigi and said, Maddie is standing right here in front of me. Maddie stepped out where Gigi could see her within the threshold.

He turned, walking away reminding her that she had her instructions. Bryan just kept walking toward the living room.

Gigi yelled at Bryan, "WHAT IS WRONG WITH YOU?", and then screeching, "IT'S CHRISTMAS!"

Bryan stopped walking. Turning, he calmly, yet loudly stated, "You... are what is wrong with this Christmas... and every prior birthday and holiday. Change your behavior 'Miss Psychology', and you will be welcomed again. You heard my instructions, get your things, and get out of my home... NOW."

By now, Gigi was spewing profanity. Maddie looked directly at Gigi, who was standing in her bedroom yelling like a child. Maddie laughed and said, "You... look... ridiculous." Maddie then turned and walked back toward the family in the living room.

...................................................................................................

There had been fifteen minutes of silence. Gigi hadn't walked out of their bedroom. Bryan decided it was time to go back in there to check and see her progress. When he got to the doorway without entering, there, sitting on the side of his bed was Gigi with a stunned look. Looking up and over toward Bryan, she started tearing up and said, "Oh my God, I've become our Dad."

Gigi burst into tears. Burying her head in her hands, her body shook with an uncontrollable sob. Bryan wasn't fooled by this act. She had done this act before. So, Bryan reminded her of this.

"HMM, I think the 2006 performance was much, much better. You really should hone your acting skills. Just a reminder Gigi, I told you to get your things and get out of my home. Nothing will be solved this Christmas." Then, turning to walk away, he projected down the hallway, "I would hate to have to call the police... possibly losing your JOB" then immediately looking back for her reaction.

Like magic, the tears were gone. This reinforced Bryan's suspicions that she was playing upon their emotional baggage.

Gigi finally spoke, "Well, do you want to talk about this? ... or what?"

"Why? YOU'RE the COUNSELOR! You called my daughter 'FAT GIRL'. My daughter is not fat... you may be, but she's not."

Maddie was now standing beside Bryan, beaming from ear to ear. She whispered 'I love you' to Bryan, while Bryan turned to her, grinned, and winked.

Ava, who was now standing at the end of the hallway spoke up "Daddy, I know I'm not fat. Aunt Gigi is just mean. Mommy said she says stuff like that just to get attention... and because she can't afford a Psychic." At that moment, Maddie turned beet red from embarrassment whispering "Psychiatrist" to Bryan.

Right when Ava finished, Bryan walked over to Ava, squatted down, and looked her right in the eyes. He said, "Sweetie, I would never, ever, ever, ever hurt you. I love you so much, I would die for you! You and your Mommy are my whole world. I love, love, love you to the moon and back!"

Bryan picked Ava up, bear hugged her and spun her around. Ava started giggling saying, "Daddy, faster... DON'T stop!"

Maddie stood watching the two of them. With her right hand on her chest, Maddie teared up from watching how much Bryan adored their daughter. Standing behind Maddie was an angry Gigi, who pushed her aside, marched out of the room, and up the stairs.

Bryan was putting Ava down on the ground when everyone heard the door slamming upstairs. Ava said, "OOOOOO, Daddy... she's in trouble. You're not supposed to slam doors in the house... you get a spanking... are you going to spank Aunt Gigi?"

Bryan grinned. Looking over at Maddie, Bryan replied, "Not today, Ava... not today."

# GOOD GHOSTS

It was the last day of October and Carolina was excited about her Class Halloween Party. Wendy had dropped her off at school dressed in her powder blue 'Glinda the Good Witch' ball gown.

After school, Carolina marched straight from the bus into Paul's work office. Plopping down in the tufted leather chair facing him, she crossed her arms, and in an adamant matter-of-fact tone said, "Daddy, some people are crazy. I'm not." Then, lowering her chin with eyes darting side to side, and a concerned look and tone, "I know I'm not."

The first thing to know about Carolina is that she is not imaginative. There is not one bone in her body that has imagination. Since birth, Carolina has kept it logical and real. She has questioned everything since she started completing sentences. Paul even joked that someday, she's going to make a great Lawyer or a superb grammar Teacher.

So, when she began telling this fantastic story about how she would wake up some nights scared or terrified, only to be calmed down by a ghost named ChiChi... Paul was willing to listen and try to believe her. Apparently during that day's classroom discussion about ghosts and goblins, Carolina had begun debating her Teacher about whether ghosts were fake or real. And, if Carolina has been calmed down by a ghost, then in her mind, they must be real.

"Ms. Schueler said that you can't touch or feel them. She doesn't know what she's talking about. ChiChi hugs me all the time! And I've always known she's a ghost."

Then with a certainty of concrete, Carolina asked Paul when ChiChi died. Paul's flabbergasted look must have angered her because she sternly questioned why he was looking at her that way. Sheepishly, he told her that normally he didn't believe in ghosts. Paul had no idea how to answer her question. Well, that's when his silence started a river of tears. With earnest and frustration, Carolina kept telling him that she knows ChiChi is real because she's hugged her.

Paul still didn't know what to say or do. He just told her to come over to him. He picked her up, sat her in his lap, kissed her forehead and hugged her. He told her that he loved her and that he believed everything she was saying. With a pouting look, Carolina sniffed. Then while gasping for air, she replied, "You don't believe me", and then with back-to-back gasps, "I can tell you don't believe me." Then Carolina buried her sobbing face into his chest.

While Paul held and rocked his sobbing daughter, he knew that he wasn't going to be finishing any spreadsheets for the meeting tomorrow. So, Paul did something he had never done before. He sent an email to his team, his boss, and his two co-workers asking if they wouldn't mind moving the meeting to Friday morning to get all the data compiled. Within 60 seconds, every single person had replied yes. Each yes followed with they could hear his daughter sobbing, and he needed to take the poor girl home.

So, home they went.

........................................................................................

When Paul and Carolina walked in the front door, Wendy was simultaneously hanging up her phone saying "Thank you for letting me know. I will talk to her."

With that, Carolina started crying again. Paul told her to go ahead and run upstairs and put on her play clothes.

"Why are you home so early. I was about to go to your office and get her so we could talk about what happened at school."

20

Paul looked up at the top of the staircase, sternly saying "Carolina... clothes". Paul lowered his voice telling Wendy they needed to talk about this in his office. They moved quickly because they knew Carolina would be back downstairs in a flash.

Paul started by explaining what happened at work. Wendy kept interrupting and interjecting with information from Ms. Schueler. So, the big picture was starting to form that either Carolina believed that a ghost was keeping her safe, or she was making the whole thing up.

That's when Paul said 'ChiChi'.

Wendy's face went completely void of color. Her eyes bulged with a combination of fear and confusion. Wendy asked Paul to clarify what name he said...

"You... said... ChiChi? You know that ChiChi was MY Grandma. She raised me. She never met Carolina. You know I don't speak about her. It just hurts too much. It was so..."

Paul grabbed Wendy. "I know... I remember. When she said that name, I kinda freaked out. But I couldn't show my fear or excitement!"

Wendy was now sobbing in Paul's chest. Carolina was now standing in the doorway.

In a terrified tremble, Carolina spoke. "Mom... is everything ok? What's wrong?"

Wendy couldn't say anything. She just turned, ran over to Carolina, grabbing her and holding her tightly. With tears streaming down both of their faces, Wendy pulled back, holding Carolina's face in her hands saying over and over, "She's seen you! Oh MY GOD! Oh my, GOD! She's seen you!"

Wendy couldn't control her sobbing. She was about to start hyperventilating when Carolina asked "Who?"

Wendy started laughing.

Wendy took Carolina by the hand and led her to the living room. Wendy pointed at the couch saying, "Sit right there". Wendy walked over to the bookcase next to the front windows. Pulling out several albums and a large wicker box from one of the cabinets, she slowly started walking backwards toward the couch.

Wendy turned and stacked each of the albums on the large coffee table. Then, by placing the large wicker box on top, gravity took over and that darn box slid off.

Out of the box fell a framed picture, making Wendy jump in panic? Carolina screamed "CHICHI!" And just like that, Wendy was crying again. With her voice cracking, "Yes... that's my ChiChi! I guess she's your ChiChi too!"

# GRAVE HOPPING

It's hard to believe...

It had been almost six months since Mom and Dad died. We finally decided to start closing things out. You know... purging, saving, donating... all with plans to sell the house. We all felt like we needed to be there when making decisions. Well, that's not entirely true. Our brother Jack, our designated family CPA, usually only cared about the money. That is, if there's enough money, and how we're going to get more of it.

So, for the first time since the funeral, we were all there together for the long weekend. Yes, we were all there... all of us together... in Mom and Dad's house... alone.

Friday morning, our two oldest brothers got up early and went down to the bank to empty out Mom and Dad's safety deposit box. When Jim and Jerre returned from the bank, I could tell something was up.

Jerre marched into the living room, threw a large file box on the coffee table, and broke the glass inserts. Just like most of our lives, our oldest brother Jim, started yelling at him. Jim is the self-appointed disciplinarian. The problem is, Mom and Dad raised five very different people.

Let's be clear, my two oldest brothers, the twins, and myself were all born ten months apart. We are all close in age. But the two oldest brothers are total opposites in personality. But never be mistaken, those two brothers are best friends. Whenever it comes to anything outside of themselves, they are always united. That's why we knew this was different. Their body language said they were divided. Jim seemed melancholy and Jerre seemed irritated.

Jack, along with his twin sister Jacklyn, reacted with anger. The two of them have always defended Jerre, even when he's wrong. I guess I inherited my Mom's temperament. As a 3$^{rd}$ Grade Teacher, I made everyone sit down and be quiet.

I calmly stood up and simply asked why tempers were so high. I started by asking Jim what happened. Like usual, Jerre tried to interrupt, which I quelled. Even though I am the youngest, I seem to always have to be firm with my siblings.

Jim began to talk about the bank box. Dad had always told tall tales about our great grandfather. Dad had promised himself to take responsibility for buying the headstone for his Grandfather's grave.

An exasperated Jerre yanked a clipping from the box dated May 12, 1935. The Article listed our Great Grandfather as a Bank Robbing Murderer. And if there was any doubt that it was him, there was a mugshot picture from jail on the front page. It also said he and his Mistress had been wounded during a 1934 robbery down in South Texas. Together, they narrowly escaped the law in a shootout across State lines to go into hiding. He wasn't heard from again until his death in 1935. He died in the arms of his wounded Mistress, who was subsequently arrested and jailed in Wink, Texas.

The Article concluded by saying that funeral arrangements were pending. Memorials could be made in lieu of flowers to the Leona Methodist Church Endowment Fund.

Jack said, "Wink, Wink", and winked at us.

Suddenly best friends again, Jerre asked Jim "Do we know anyone in Wink? Wait, isn't that when the church bought the land for the new building?". This started a fifteen-minute family discussion of our family's church patronage. Comically, even though we were all wondering, no one revisited the subjects of Wink, nor the Mistress.

I was trying to figure out what the big deal was and wondering how to get us back on track. Jacklyn wouldn't look at me. I needed her help. I kept staring at her like "HELP ME!" and then she finally saw my exasperation and abruptly pointed at me and said "Wait... what did you say?" Finally, we were back on track.

With my transition, Jim started all over again. But now, we kind of knew where he was heading. He said that since Dad is now dead, it's our responsibility to find Great Grandad's grave. It became obvious that Jim wanted us to bear this responsibility as our duty to give Great Grandad a proper headstone.

Jim sadly looked at me, with pitiful, puppy dog eyes. Then he pointed at some jotted notes on a faded yellow notepad. Then in a tone of desperation, Jim said "We'll use these coins to pay for it", dumping a flour-sack full of coins on the coffee table. Those coins covered most of the table... barely missing the new hole created by the broken glass.

Leave it to Jack to notice what type of coins they were. "Aren't those silver dollars?" The note with them said there were 126 Morgan Silver Dollars.

Jack continued by saying "FINALLY... we could be rich and have to give it to a dead man, a masonry, and a block of granite! It's like a terrible joke."

Of course, Jerre and Jacklyn agreed, but for once, I aligned with Jim... for Dad's sake.

So, with a deep breath, I picked up the notepad and looked at the location of the grave. "This is actually doable".

With a little disdain, Jack said: "Aren't ya'll just a wee pit curious how much those silver dollars are worth?... I mean, come on! Just a little?"

A little disgruntled, Jim replied that of course we were all curious. But Jim pointed out that Dad wanted to do this. Dad adored this Grandad. Even if it was partially out of folklore, what better way to honor Dad, and the Grandad he knew? This would be like fulfilling his final request.

Jacklyn and I were looking at the directions for the grave location. We noticed it was over on Uncle Bubba's property. It was just past our family cemetery hill. Then I suggested we take a little drive out there.

Just like that, Jim was calling Uncle Bubba to warn him, and we were all piling into Jack's Suburban. Here we were, in our 40's and 50's, on some Teenage adventure. In honor of Mom, we decided to run through Sonic for a Cherry-Limeade for the 'road-trip'.

Jim said he thought Dad would have loved being in the car with us. Of course, Jerre started razzing him on being overly sensitive.

Driving out there, we realized how much the topography had changed over the past twenty years. New wind turbines, energy windmills and solar panel farms were everywhere... and then, we turned off onto Uncle Bubba's dirt road. Jim said he told Uncle Bubba we were going to go Grave Hopping.

We didn't stop or even slow down at the Cemetery entrance. The directions said that once we cleared the cemetery gate, take a wide curve to the right, and then turn back to the left. There should be a creek surrounded by trees. A twisty path lead from the road to the trees lining the creek. Where that path ends, that's where the grave is marked to be. And just like the directions said, we were almost at the creek when we saw a twisty path. Trees lined the creek, so Jack stopped at the end of the road where he went ahead and parked under one of the shade trees.

We all piled out and started walking toward the creek. Our crudely drawn map showed a V shaped path. Like when we were kids, I grabbed Jacklyn's hand, started skipping while singing 'Follow the Yellow Brick Road' as the guys walked. We were out of breath quickly from the heat, but we were too busy laughing to care.

We veered right a little and then took a sharp left for 9 or so feet. We came to a large group of shade trees, and then counted the third from the right of the path.

Jacklyn screamed, "There it is". So, we rushed to the tree, stopped, and looked down. With a collective sigh, we all said "OH."

There it was, just as plain as the daylight sun.

Flat on the ground was a cement marker with the inscription:

"Here lies the Father of many

the Husband of a Loyal, Faithful, Christian Wife.

May you rot in Hell for all Eternity

YOU CHEATING BASTARD."

A stoic Jim, bowed his head, crossed his arms in front of him and said, "I think that says it all."

..............................................................................................

For the record, Uncle Bubba bought those Morgan Silver Dollars for 3000 bucks. Divided by five... I'd say we're finally rich.

# HOUSE ON THE CREEK

Nikki said she had always wanted to live in a small town. So, when my promotion moved me to Bowie, Texas, Nikki declared that this would be our forever home. It was the perfect small town to raise our future kids. The next thing she did was set her focus on finding the perfect house for us to renovate. We immediately rented an apartment and began the hunt for an old 'fixer-upper'.

For almost a year, we had stomped around town and outlying areas. I was about to get irritated and just tell Nikki that any house would suffice. That's when Nikki called me at work. It was late one afternoon, and her excitement was leaping through the phone.

Nikki said she had run into Mrs. Scoggins from church down at Brookshire's grocery store. Nikki was helping her get something off the top shelf when they started talking. Nikki can make conversation with anyone. Apparently, they started with religion, turning to children, grandchildren, dead spouses, all leading to our housing situation. Nikki even told her she was getting depressed, and even regretting moving to Bowie.

Then Ms. Scoggins said she had the best idea! She owned an old farmhouse just outside of town. She warned that no one had lived there since the early forties, and it was only used maybe once or twice a year for family get-togethers. She also said that everyone in the family was tired of trying to keep it up. She reassured Nikki that she'd check with her family to see if they'd be willing to sell it and then give us a call. I could hear Nikki's voice bounce with excitement.

I hadn't realized I've missed that bounce. It's been a while since I've heard that in Nikki's voice. I knew she needed this... and then, in a concerned tone, Nikki said, "Oh yeah. It's on a creek". Of course, I went silent!

Nikki knows how much I hate snakes. So, I said, "Did you say… it's on a snake… I mean a creek?" Nikki was so excited about owning a house on a creek, it's like she didn't process what I said. I couldn't understand why on Earth she would want to live somewhere that might or might not attract snakes.

So, with my fears exposed, I started asking rhetorical questions. "You do know that snakes like water? In fact, they love water. And did you know that water moccasins can climb trees? Yes, they can… and they'll chase you.  And what happens if we renovate that old house, and we start having kids and they get bit by a snake? Hey, it could happen! And I really don't want that on my conscience." Nikki told me to calm down and take a deep breath.

Three days later, once again, Nikki called me at work. This time it was 8:05 in the morning. "House 5 thousand dollars; land is 10". Not a 'Hello', or 'Hi, it's me, your wife Nikki'… just a cash amount and silence. Then she said condescendingly, "Hello? Are you there?… Well, I told her we'd take it!"

OK honestly, I hadn't been reacting well at home. I will admit it, now. When she called and said, "We'd take it", I sort of exploded (much to my co-worker's chagrin). My volume and panic were heard throughout the work office.

I started venting that we hadn't even seen the place! We don't know where it is, nor what kind of condition it's in! What if we need to commission snake exterminators? I was not going to live in a place with all those snakes… the bottom line is we have no idea what we could be getting into, and we don't know if we can afford it.

Nikki's anger was immediate. My fears and my doubts sent her into orbit. "So, if it's your idea, it's great… if it's my idea, it's not? Is that what you're trying to say here? That my ideas SUCK and what I want doesn't matter? As long as YOU'RE happy… Well, IS IT? Oh, and by the way, put on your big-boy pants and grow a pair!"

I immediately knew there was no good way out of this, so I just agreed to disagree. I swallowed what little pride I had left and said we would go look at the 'house of snakes' tomorrow.

Then, Nikki turned on her charm. "It'll be ok. You trust me, don't you? And you know Mrs. Scoggins from church. She's so sweet. You love her. She wouldn't steer us wrong." Then, Nikki tried to play a 'spade' by saying "she reminds me of your late Grandmother."

My first thought was 'that was manipulative'. My second thought was that Satan's Minions seem sweet at first too, especially when they want something. It was like I started questioning whether my wife had joined a Satanic Snake Cult. "What if the Snake Cult wants to eat our first-born child?" I suddenly realized I said that with my outside voice. That's when Nikki became furious with me. So, because I am a typical guy who doesn't know when to quit, I took it one step too far.

"Is your head spinning around now?"

....................................................................................................

So that afternoon, instead of tomorrow, we were on our way to see the 'snake house' on the creek.

In the car, Nikki was relatively quiet and only giving directions. First, we turned off Highway 287 at the Armadillo and headed the wrong direction. We turned, veered, and turned down some dirt road. Then we turned again, and again, driving down more dirt and gravel roads.

I started complaining. Yes, I sounded like a whining child. This started another argument. In my mind, I kept thinking, 'the further we get from town, the more I hate this place'. And then with each new dirt road, I brought up rain and mud, and getting stuck out here in the middle of nowhere. My attitude shifted from bad to worse. However, Nikki was throwing it right back at me.

And then, in the middle of this 'I'm right, you're wrong' argument, Nikki squealed. Scaring me half-to-death, I almost ran off the gravel road and into the bar-ditch! Then, she started tearing up like she was about to cry. She pointed and said, "I bet that's it".

Not helping matters, I replied with sarcasm.

"What gave it away... the people waving at us?"

By the look I got, I knew I had to change my attitude and my behavior. Nikki was done with my pedantic antics.

When we finally stopped behind Mrs. Scoggins big, brown Cadillac, Nikki scolded me. In a tone I had never heard her use, she yelled, "THAT'S IT..." Looking down, staring at my waist, and then back up to my eyes, she stared with eyes slanted like a snake. Firmly, she stated "If you give me any more lip, you're CUT off". From that look, I knew what she meant.

Now, there standing before us was Mrs. Scoggins and her Grandson Jeff. Jeff just happened to be one of my old college buddies. Seeing Jeff, my attitude was miraculously transformed. It turned out that the little old lady from Brookshire's was his Grandma.

After we reconnected and shouted to the world that we knew each other, I piped up about the 'snake house' scenario. Jeff started belly laughing. "Grannie... it's not on a creek! It's near a creek, but not on a creek!"

Nikki's beaming smile completely collapsed, and she started crying. I took her hand, grinned and winked at her saying, "Hey, it's ok. We'll get it anyway and we'll put in a creek."

Incidentally, the house was great... big kitchen, big porch, big bedrooms, big everything... except for bathrooms and closets. With all that space, those things can be fixed.

I asked Jeff if they were serious about the total 15k? He said it was important to his Grannie that it be a permanent home, and that Nikki had that look in her eyes. I started laughing because at that moment, Nikki was staring at the staircase. I pointed at her questioning, "Was that the look?". We all started laughing, especially Nikki. That's when Ms. Scoggins shocked me by turning to Nikki and asking, "Now tell me again sweetie, when are ya'll due?".

# I KNEW THERE WAS A GOD!

Patty had just finished putting the final decorations up in our old High School Cafeteria. On the way out, she called me to tell me that Baby T had texted her, and that she would definitely be there tonight.

Tonight, was our High School Reunion.

Baby T is Teresa's nickname. She was the youngest in our class, so we called her Baby T. She was funny, round, and one of my best friends through grade school. Honestly, growing up, we all struggled with our weight, but Baby T seemed to struggle more than anyone else. Even through High School, the three of us were considered 'a bit heavy'. Three years ago, Patty told me that Baby T had undergone Gastric Bypass Surgery.

At our last reunion, Baby T was having a hard time breathing and sitting on the tiny metal chairs. She leaned over and whispered to me that she was now over 400 pounds. Then, Baby T added that just watching prissy Jaclyn prance and swish around the cafeteria, made her want to vomit and poke her eyes out.

OH Jaclyn. If anyone could wish harm upon anyone, she'd be the one you'd wish it upon. Since we were in the 4th grade, Jaclyn has always Lorded being 'beautiful' over us. In fact, even the Parents, Teachers, and visitors from other schools would point and discuss her beauty. And if you needed more proof, she was fourth runner-up Miss Texas. And as for the Miss Texas Pageant, I can't even imagine what our small town would have done had she actually won. The City Council would probably erect a giant Billboard just outside of town saying, "Home of Miss Texas"! Then they'd slap her big Head and Crown up there for the world to see. Talk about distracting... I might have to hurl my car off the freeway toward a blunt object!

But as all small-town people know, the rumor mill is always working over-time. The rumor around town was that she would have won the whole pageant if she hadn't been so stuck up and tacky to the 'ugly' people. Her Mom said that everyone was just intimidated by her great beauty, making a reference to how Elizabeth Taylor must have felt. Sadly, from personal experience dealing with Jaclyn, I am prone to believe the rumor mill over what her Mother claimed down at the Junior League.

In fact, I remember one of the many times in High School where Jaclyn made me want to punch her in her vanity. Our class was decorating for Junior Prom, in the very cafeteria where we hold our reunions.

We needed every available hand in that room to help lift the wire and attach it to each wall in the room. We were about to put in a dropped paper ceiling when I asked her to help. Jaclyn turned to me, looked me directly in my eyes and said, "I don't have to." Then I asked her why and she replied, "Because I'm pretty."

WHAT? WHO SAYS THAT? In what alternative Universe does she live? Who does she think she is... Miss Texas? She hadn't lost the pageant... YET. With my typical reaction, I just rolled my eyes, and walked away.

Where she was snotty and condescending to me, she was mean to Baby T. Baby T has always hated Jaclyn, and for good reason. I don't know why she was always bullying her. First, Jaclyn would follow her around the playground. Then she started following her up and down hallways oinking and mooing. Then, she started making squishing sounds, followed by thumping and pounding sounds as Baby T walked anywhere. Every time she would think of a new sound, or any other hateful 'fat' noises, she would heap them upon Baby T. But I think the worst thing was calling her Lard Butt. Kids are so cruel, and of course, Lard Butt is the nickname which stuck.

Well, regardless of Jaclyn, I must admit that I was excited about our reunion. Patty and I got to the High School early enough to grab the seats we wanted. Patty said that Baby T was bringing her new husband. Years ago, I stopped trying to keep up with Baby T and all her drama. I didn't even know that Baby T had gotten re-married.

So, after the first hour of the Reunion, that's when Baby T walked in the door. I didn't even recognize her. She looked amazing. And her new husband was a total Hunk. She took his arm strolling around the cafeteria. It was like she thought she was a Duchess greeting her peasants. Everyone in the room were drooling. If I'm being honest, I was truly happy for her. She finally got to be the 'Bell of the Ball'.

Well, the night was almost over. Baby T had gone to go get us some punch. Suddenly, Baby T came running back to the table. I had never seen her run, so this was rather shocking. Out of breath and panting, she said with absolute glee "Oh... My... GAWD."

Baby T continued: "I always knew there was a God, but now, we have proof. WE HAVE PROOF! He answered our prayers from the 4th grade! First... Jaclyn is divorced... YES! The Star Quarterback dropped her for someone YOUNGER! Second... SHE'S FAT! Oh, my GAWD, SHE'S FAT!!! BEAUTY QUEEN JACLYN IS FAT! See, see, I knew there was a GOD!!!"

I kept trying to get Baby T to quiet down, but she just kept saying it, over and over, and getting louder and louder.

Then, Baby T... Teresa, saw my eyes tearing up and she stopped speaking.

As Baby T slowly turned, standing behind her new, shapely figure stood a very large Jaclyn. Jaclyn nodded and said with a remorse I swore I would never hear, "I know I deserved that..." and she turned and walked away.

Teresa's face fell, and her eyes started tearing up. Looking up and shaking her head, Teresa spun on her heels and followed after Jaclyn. Baby T slightly grabbed her arm, took her hand in her own and said "No, actually you didn't deserve that; no one deserves that treatment."

The two of them started crying and hugged each other while the music continued, and never skipped a beat.

That's when Patty leaned over to me and asked, "Does this mean that Baby T has gone over to the dark side?"

# MALCOLM AND LUCRETIA: 2013

"Are you ok?"

"Yes. Just looking out the window...thinking about everything."

"Anything wrong?"

"OH NO. Everything is perfect... actually, better than perfect."

Lucretia stood staring out the window. The view of downtown was impressive. This was the first outing they had taken since Malcolm's Father passed away. She couldn't wait for tonight.

Right then, her cell phone rang.

"Who would be calling you on New Year's Eve?"

"I don't know. Ohhh... I've been hoping..."

She went ahead and answered the phone "Hello? Yes. OH... ok, thanks for letting me know." There was a small pause, and she continued "So, everything looked ok?... Yes, thank you for letting me know... I was a bit concerned, but now... it's all great. Thank you again... and, and, thanks for calling me on New Year's Eve... Bye... and, and take care."

Turning to Malcolm, she said "That was my Doctor."

"Are you ok?"

She shook her head yes, smiled, and turned back toward the view. Changing the subject, she told Malcolm she was excited about dinner tonight, and that he did good on selecting the Hotel and that the view was amazing. She turned around slowly. Her eyes danced and her smile was beaming. Then, her face turned to a look of slight concern.

"OK... I think I'm ready to tell you."

Malcolm's relief and happy look shifted to a more concerned look.

Lucretia continued, "Look, don't worry sweetie. It's nothing... except... I love you."

"Oh goodness... for a second you had me worried. Well... first, I know you love me... but then I was getting worried, like that phone call was cancer... or something scarier. Don't do that to me again."

"What?"

"I don't know. In that one instant, your tone sent me from happy to fear... or something... I don't quite know... it was a feeling."

"WHAT? So, my tone is a Superpower? I must have some powerful vibes. I just wanted to thank you for loving me. It's been a tough year. I think we're ready for 2013."

"I think you're right. Actually, I know you're right."

Malcolm started to laugh, then stopped again "OK... what's going on? Your look just changed again."

Smiling while shaking her head, she said, "Look, I'm over 40 now. I've been assessing my life..." followed by snickering "through the window."

"Well, I've been over 50 for almost a year now! Was I supposed to assess my life too?" Looking into each other's eyes, they both started breath laughing.

Then, as their air laughter turned into a belly laugh, their eyes danced with each other. Ten years of marriage, eight years of trying for kids... and finally, their number one bucket list item, 'The Ball Drop'.

The night started flying by. Malcolm and Lucretia dressed up, and warm. Then, they went to their dinner reservations down the street from Times Square, finally heading out to join the millions of people out in the New York streets.

Up until twenty minutes before the Ball dropped, the two could actually hear each other speak. Then gradually, a roar started developing. By the time the Ball was counting down minutes, the noise level was so loud, they could feel the vibrations in their chests.

With 30 seconds left in 2012, Lucretia had to tell him.

He had to know right now. This New Year had to start off right... So, Lucretia grabbed his face and yelled "I'm PREGNANT". He couldn't hear what she said.

The seconds were ticking too fast. Lucretia started to panic... He couldn't hear her.

Yelling again, but much louder, "I'M PREGNANT" ... She started tearing up because he kept looking at her with a blank look saying "What?" ...

Lucretia started freaking out! This was a true panic. She had to do something...

"10", she grabbed his hand...

"8" she held it on her stomach...

"6" while shaking her head up and down... and making him look into her teary eyes...

And then on "2" ... he finally knew...

..................................................................................................

Later that night, after the two had returned to their room, Lucretia was once again standing at the window. Malcolm questioned her once again.

"You ok?"

"Are you?"

"Are you kidding me? I'm gonna be a Dad! And I got to see the ball drop!"

"No, you didn't... your back was to it... you couldn't see it."

"Yes, I could... I saw it in your eyes."

# NANCY AND T-ANNE

For almost ten years, Nancy and T-Anne had been together in a Bible Study. Before yesterday, Nancy could have counted on one hand the number of words T-Anne had spoken every Tuesday. Most words were yes, no, or just a blank stare. But every week, for ten years, T-Anne faithfully showed up and was present for each Study.

Several weeks ago, Nancy brought up Thanksgiving. Each year between Thanksgiving and Christmas, they rotated hosting duties. Most of the members of the group volunteered to host one week. Being the Preacher's wife, Nancy hosted the majority of the year, and this gave her a much-needed break. Nancy always resumed hosting duties beginning with a great big Christmas "shindig"!

This year, the week before Thanksgiving, Nancy once again asked for volunteers to host. For the first time, T-Anne spoke up! "I'll do the week after Thanksgiving!"

With glee, Nancy said, "That's great! Thank you! I can't wait to see your place!", with T-Anne replying, "I just finished restoring, renovating, and reorganizing. So now, the house is starting to feel like a real home."

In a matter of a couple of minutes, T-Anne had put together more words than she had spoken in each of the last ten years. She even volunteered to take care of everything, including food, beverages, and desserts.

So, when the day finally arrived, everyone showed up excited. T-Anne's beautiful Historical Home was situated on Main Street. For over ten years, everyone had watched as T-Anne transformed her home from an eyesore into a glamorous image from the past. Their excitement showed as each of them bounced up the grand steps. As each member arrived, T-Anne gave a guided tour. She told each person the history of the home. She also told them what was restored and what as renovated; about the families who had previously owned the house, and how each prior family were ironically connected by church. After each tour, the remaining members would gather in T-Anne's vast, formal living room, talking about T-Anne and her home.

During all of this, Nancy realized they really didn't know much about T-Anne. It wasn't until this day that they realized how funny and interesting T-Anne was, and how knowledgeable she was when it came to History and restoration.

It was finally time to eat and begin Bible Study. There was a renewed energy that permeated through the group. T-Anne continued to serve the tiny tea sandwiches she had made, and refilling exotic Gobi punch, iced-cookies, and chocolate chip pound cake. They discussed how difficult Holidays can be; through it all, the women laughed and cried. This was by far the best Bible Study they had ever experienced.

At T-Anne 's suggestion, they decided as a group to volunteer down at the Women's Shelter. Nancy and all the members were moved to tears. There was a new sense of purpose that had developed. As everyone was leaving, each one gushed how wonderful Bible Study had been. Nancy moved back to the Kitchen and started washing dishes to help T-Anne clean up. When everyone had left, T-Anne walked into the Kitchen.

"Nancy, you don't have to do that... I really don't mind cleaning up. I love entertaining. In fact, I forgot how much I love doing it."

Nancy couldn't control her emotions. Tearing up, she turned to T-Anne. "I just want you to know that I love you."

T-Anne was taken aback and started tearing up herself.

Nancy continued through tears, "This is the first time in over ten years I feel like you really wanted to be here. 1Is it because... well, is it our race? Did you not trust us? Well, until now? Well... well, I mean... I understand if that's the case... and everything around here..." Exasperated with sadness, Nancy finished by saying, "well, you know..."

With a great big sigh T-Anne said, "I couldn't..."; and with big crocodile tears forming, T-Anne walked over and hugged Nancy and saying with her voice cracking, "I love you too." Taking her hand, T-Anne said, "Come with me" as she led her back to the living room, stopping in front of the Fireplace.

There, perched on the right side of the Mantel was a gold framed, white canvas. There was no image, no picture... nothing. No one said a word about it because the house was so lovely. Considering this was the first time each of them had been invited into her house, they certainly didn't want to hurt or offend her in any way. Plus, T-Anne had been the most open and gracious hostess.

So, there they stood, staring at the blank canvas, together. T-Anne turned to Nancy. Tears rolling down her face. "For self-diagnosed therapy, I painted this over a hundred times." Then, with a slight snicker and rolling her eyes, T-Anne said, "This is my final result."

Nancy leaned in and looked more closely at it. It was white, wispy swirls. She said, "It looks like clouds of cotton. It's absolutely beautiful."

Then T-Anne continued. "Ten years ago, I had to move back here to put my Mom in that Nursing Home. Well, that's not completely true. Mom had full on dementia. But that's not why I moved back. I could have moved her to Shreveport. That's where me and my Husband settled after graduating from college. My family had lived there for almost twenty years. But now... my family is dead."

"WHAT?" Nancy looked with horror. "What do you mean?", as she grabbed T-Anne 's hand again.

"It started with my Husband. He hurt his back teaching our daughter to ride a horse. He just needed something to get through the day, so he went to the Doctor. Then after a year and a half, his pain killer usage had escalated."

T-Anne continued, "It was obvious that he was addicted. So, his Doctor confronted him that he was concerned about his developing problem. Of course, he denied it. So that's when he started drinking with the pills. After a while, he started going to the bar. He said he was tired of me 'nagging' him about his behavior."

Nancy's concern was obvious. She replied "Oh, no. That's a lethal combo."

Then T-Anne started really divulging her past. "Then my little girl, who wasn't so little anymore, wanted to recruit kids for Vacation Bible School. I would take her and her girlfriends from church and drop them off at the end of different blocks. I was so proud of them as they would go door to door inviting so many people."

"On one block, some older white man started yelling at my daughter. He told her to get her black butt off his property. His next-door neighbor, who just happened to be watering his lawn, over-heard him yelling at her and saying that he was going to go grab his gun. He was threatening my twelve-year-old daughter with a gun. A grown man was threatening my twelve-year-old daughter because she was black. All she wanted to do was invite the neighborhood kids to VBS."

Pausing for a moment, she continued, "By now, most of the neighbors had come out of their homes to see what all the

46

commotion was about. Just like them, I had just gotten out of my car to see what was going on.  That's when we heard him screaming at her. My terrified daughter started running away from him. When I saw him lunge at her, that's when she looked back, and tripped. I watched her as she fell and hit her head on his curb."

T-Anne paused again, took a deep breath saying, "She died that evening at the Hospital. I saw the whole thing..." Shaking her head and repeating, "I saw the whole thing."

T-Anne was no longer crying. As she spoke, she simply displayed a vacant, sad, matter-of-fact tone saying "I can't cry anymore about it... I just can't", as she started tearing up again.

Nancy broke the silent pause, "OH, you poor thing! Where was your Husband? Oh, I shouldn't have asked that... that's none of my business."

T-Anne answered her: "It's ok. I haven't spoken about it to anyone in so long, I probably need too."

"And as for my Husband, at first he couldn't remember. But when I pointed out that he had lipstick all over him and smelled of a woman's perfume, he came clean about his affair. So, in one night, I lost my daughter and my marriage."

Nancy stood in silence.  Her mouth hung open, and her face was visibly shocked. Then innocently, Nancy asked, "How did y'all get through it?"

With a contemplative look and partially biting her bottom lip, T-Anne paused and then said, "He committed suicide", and then looking back at Nancy finishing, "and I moved home to Texas."

"He WHAT?" Nancy yelped.

T-Anne was frank about it saying, "He took the easy way out... well, for him it was easy. It wasn't easy for any of us he left

47

behind." Then, emphasizing the word little, T-Anne said, "I guess you can tell I'm still a little angry that he left me to deal with everything."

Nancy grabbed T-Anne, bear hugging her and squeezing her as tight as she could muster. Suddenly, T-Anne lost it. She started sobbing uncontrollably.

With her voice cracking, T-Anne spoke with her face pressed into Nancy's shoulder, "It's just been so hard... and one minute, I want to kill him, and the next minute... I just want him to hold me." Then, with an almost convulsion, T-Anne murmured, "I just want Mike to tell me that it's going to be ok."

Still holding T-Anne and with tears rolling down both their cheeks, Nancy leaned back, looking at T-Anne. With hope in her teary eyes and a slight smile, Nancy said "Ya know what? It's all going to be ok."

Still sniffing and slightly heaving, T-Anne looked directly at Nancy. Hugging her just a little tighter, T-Anne started weeping again. Through her tears, and a slight smile from a newfound friendship, T-Anne said, "I know it's going to be ok... It's not ok right now, but I know it will be."

# RACE OF THE CENTURY

Dewayne had forgotten about his own experience with Cub Scouts. It wasn't until he heard his own Father's words come out of his mouth to his own son saying, "The ONLY place Success comes before Work, is in the Dictionary!"

He couldn't believe it when he heard himself. Dewayne guessed that the phrase 'History Repeats Itself' was beating him in the face. Every memory came rushing back. Dewayne ran to the phone, calling his Dad, and both started laughing. Of course, Willie J wasn't laughing.

In an angry tone, Willie J said: "Dad, what's so funny?".

Laughing, Dewayne turned toward Willie J and said, "Kid, go ahead and hate me today, but this is your race, not mine. You're gonna make your own race car. And in 20 years, you're gonna say the same things to your son." Willie J was not amused and stormed off to his room.

Dewayne returned to the phone conversation with his Dad. "I bet you never thought you would hear me quote you."

Through the phone, Willie said "You know kid, I always knew you were listening. Hey, look how good you turned out. Keep it up Kid! You're a great Dad. My Dad was always so daggum critical of me."

After they had reminisced for a while and hung up with their usual catch phrase "Love you the most!", Dewayne ventured back to Willie J's bedroom. He just wanted to see how the progress was going. There, whittling away at his little wooden block, Willie J was crafting his race car. It was way better than anything he could ever imagine or build.

"WOW! You're incredible! Mine was so bad. Yours' looks like a real car! Almost like a Pantera from the 1970's"

Dewayne had been obsessed with cars since childhood. He had no craft or mechanical ability whatsoever, but he was passionately obsessed. Where Dewayne lacked in those abilities, he was great at Math. And even though Dewayne's Dad was an Architectural Engineer, his Dad was so proud of him when he became an Accountant.

"Maybe, YOU can be an Architect or Engineer like your Grandad."

"Dad, I need to make lots of money."

At that moment, both Father and Son had that gleam in their eyes. Both began gazing at the poster of a new Bugatti framed and hung upon the wall. Of course, Dewayne had gotten it for his son when they saw it at the mall. Willie J's Mom was so angry about it. She couldn't believe that he had spent 280 dollars of their money on a framed poster. But the boys felt it was worth every penny.

After that, Dewayne returned to the living room. Plopping on the couch, he picked up his tablet to surf the internet, immediately going to the 1938 Bugatti. That was what his block was supposed to be when he finished, not that blob of a hatchet job he painted.

Still, the memories from that event were some of Dewayne's favorite memories with his Dad.

Prior to the Cub Scout Car Race, Dewayne had procrastinated for three weeks. All his friends and some of the guys at school, kept talking about how each of their Dads were helping. Some were mapping out plans on how to turn their cars into their dream cars, and some Dads just took over to create the car they wanted. Every day, Dewayne went home to the house where his Dad would say, "Kid, you gotta get to work on that car, it's not going to build itself."

Then, Friday night before the big event, Dewayne slowly walked into the Living Room, almost in tears. He looked at his Mom who had the look of disgust on her face. "Is that supposed to be your car?"

His Dad answered her by saying "Now THAT is a great Jalopy. I bet it wins the whole thing."

Dewayne gave a half grin, knowing his car resembled nothing like the MatchBox Bugatti's he had collected. He slightly shrugged his shoulders and said, "At least it's the right color" holding up his Cobalt Blue 1938 Bugatti. Sadly, he turned and walked back into his bedroom.

The next morning came sooner than later. At this point, Dewayne didn't even want to go to the race. Willie came running into his room, throwing back his covers and saying, "Today's the big day Son!" Willie had more than enough excitement for the two of them.

When they pulled up at the Scout Lodge, all other Dad's and Sons were strutting around, holding their cars like they were carrying gold from Fort Knox. Each Dad was more concerned about the car, than their Sons. Dewayne had shoved his 'car' into a shoe box used to hold his Dad's mouse traps in the garage. Willie leaned over to Dewayne, winking, and saying, "Well, they've been busy. Wonder if they used a miter saw too." Both Father and Son snickered and laughed.

Willie and Dewayne walked over and started talking with the group of Dads. None of the Sons were saying a word, just listening. It became immediately clear that their Fathers were discussing their own times as Cub Scouts. Then, one of the Dads said, "You know, Buddy's son is competing too."

Willie's dark eyes cut over to Frank's Dad. "Well, I made my son make his own, just like I did. And I won."

Dewayne's stomach started turning. He hadn't realized he was in some sort of Legacy Fight. That's when Buddy and his micro-twin walked up with their great big grins and great big teeth. They walked around the group, greeting everyone as if they had won the State Football Championship last night.

Scott, Buddy's son came running up to Dewayne telling him angrily that his Dad had hogged the entire project. He wasn't even allowed to paint any of the colors, just the clear coat so that he wouldn't mess it up.

Old Man L.L. Holden called everyone to the main room. When entering, it was like a great big Hot Wheel racetrack. Dewayne asked Mr. Holden if he could go get his Matchbox Bugatti cars to see how they'd do. Mr. Holden answered, "Son, we've got a bigger race about happen."

Dewayne started quoting all the Bugatti stats from 1938, and how no other car was comparable at that time in History. Not only was it the most beautifully crafted auto of its day, but it was also the most coveted and would now be worth several million dollars.

Mr. Holden had grown tired of Willie's Son saying, "Willie, he talks too much. Get him away from me."

It was now time to draw numbers for race order. They would compete two at a time.

Willie looked down at Dewayne and said, "Kid, you got this."

Dewayne was the last one to draw a number. Mr. Holden just handed him the number. Dewayne was eleventh out of twelve. Scott ran up to Dewayne saying, "Dad is twelve."

Numbers one and two went first, then three and four… and so on. It was now time for eleven and twelve. Everyone knew that this was war between the Dads.

Buddy yanked Scott by his arm, dragging him up to the spot where number twelve would stand. Willie turned to Dewayne and asked, "You ready?"

Buddy yelled for Willie to get his Nerd up there so he could beat him. Buddy pulled a sleek, silver car, with a fin out of a royal blue, cloth whiskey bag. Every guy in the room gasped.

"Dad... I think I'm gonna be sick.", Dewayne whispered quietly to Willie. With complete confidence, Willie turned, nodded, and smiled saying, "I told you, you've got this."

Dewayne walked over with his dusty, faded yellow shoe box. He opened it up, pulling out a jagged piece of block that looked like a rough, used door wedge. As Dewayne looked up at that gleaming, silver race car in Mr. Buddy's hands, his bottom lip started quivering, and his eyes started tearing up. Dewayne looked back down as his model car where the wheels were barely hanging onto his 'jalopy'.

Willie put his warm hand on Dewayne's back, right below his neck. Leaning over, Willie repeated, "Kid, stand up straight. You've got this."

The kids put their cars in their respective lanes. And just like that... Mr. Holden dropped the lever and off the cars went. It was over so fast, but the winner was unmistakable and witnessed by everyone.

When the lever dropped, Dewayne's pitiful little car, with its jagged edge and wobbly wheels, flung itself down the ramp. It was so hard and fast, bouncing back and forth inside its own lane, that when it hit the bottom of the slope, it took off... literally. Dewayne's car leaped off ramp. It flew off the track, launching it directly at Mr. Buddy's cheering face. Mr. Buddy had to hit the ground from getting hit between the eyes. Missing him by millimeters, Dewayne's car then finally burst through a windowpane and into the outside world of freedom. The entire room erupted to thunderous screams.

Willie grabbed Dewayne, picked him up hugging him tightly and spinning him around as the room finally quieted down.

Technically, Scott and his Dad, Mr. Buddy won their race; they even won the whole tournament. But everyone remembers that November day, when Dewayne's Bugatti took flight.

# SOME MIGHT DISAGREE

This is the story I've been told my whole life.

Firstly, there were two things the family all knew about my Grandmother. 1) Her favorite flower was the Yellow Rose; and 2) She despised vanity and always dressed in red and black.

Secondly, my Grandmother worked in a Men's Clothing Store. She dressed many of the Professionals and Executives in West Texas. She initially began working there for the discount to dress my Grandad. He was always networking. If he wasn't wheeling and dealing behind that big desk in his office, he was searching for a money-maker. Grandad built and lost five different fortunes and somehow, always managed to be one step ahead of the debt collectors. In his West Texas drawl he'd say, "It's all about leverage, kid".

This was Christmas, 1953. The house was already decorated with its usual greenery. Red and gold balls draped everything, stockings were hung, and the biggest Christmas tree Fifty dollars could buy, sat in the corner of the Formal Living Room. Grandad always had Grandmother throw the biggest Christmas party. It was ALWAYS four days before Christmas. Everyone in town knew that the party December 21st, was the invite of the season.

That year, my Grandfather had the brilliant idea to have Grandmother open his gift during the party. What better way to show this year's monetary success, and his Hollywood smile, than to impress 'the wife' in front of a large audience of peers, and some adversaries. Yes, my Grandad was arrogant... very good looking and arrogant.

Grandad had planned everything. He found the perfect gift. He even convinced the wrappers at Hemphill-Wells, the West Texas answer to Neiman Marcus, to wrap his gift. He knew that just the thought of a package from Hemphill-Wells meant

BIG MONEY. Nothing could be more impressive than a gift with that gold embossed lettering.

It was now eight o'clock and the time had finally come. Always the Master of Ceremonies, Grandfather called everyone into the foyer. He marched up and stood in the middle of the staircase. He called down to my grandmother to join him. Out of the formal living room she came to accompany him. He announced to everyone that it was gift time! Of course, my Grandmother had no idea what was to come, she was simply beaming with excitement.

With the authority a Naval ship captain, Grandad called upon my Uncle to bring in the gift. Apparently, her face, and all eyes followed that wrapped package across the room. Knowing my Grandad, this only reinforced that his instincts were correct.

Grandmother took the package. She began trying to balance this cumbersome box on her thigh.

It wasn't working, so she decided to move down the staircase to the entry table. All eyes followed her and that box as she carried it to the marble table, nodding her head at my Uncle to remove its vase. My Uncle acted quickly, grabbing, and removing the poinsettia arrangement that sat in the center.

There was barely enough room for that gift. She began to open it. When she finally got it open, she pulled out yet another wrapped object. This was obviously a picture, wrapped up like a mummy!

As she tore off each strip, an image began to appear. A puzzled look ran across her face. Finally, staring back at her, was a huge painted image of my Grandad's. It was his self-portrait.

My Grandmother's smile turned to an icy grimace. She quietly wrapped the package back up, slid it back into the box. She instructed my Uncle to carry it into Grandad's office, turned and walked out of the foyer, then stopping in front of the Living Room fireplace, slowly turning around. Now facing everyone, she smiled with a half-smile. No one could tell what she was thinking, but they knew it couldn't be good.

By evenings end, my Grandad knew he needed to 'fix this'. Those few instructions, given to my Uncle, were the last words she spoke to any family member... until January 25th... her birthday.

When Grandmother returned from work that Monday afternoon, the house seemed empty. There, standing at the front door was my Grandad. Grinning from ear to ear, he knew he had 'fixed' everything.

Grandmother paused, then entered. On the entry table sat another package... obviously another picture. With speechless disdain, my Grandmother followed instructions and began opening this crudely wrapped gift. He told her he wrapped it himself. She smirked, about to smile... until the newest image appeared.

There, staring back at Grandmother was a beautifully painted image of her engagement picture. White dress with orange polka dots... that's all she could stare at. She slowly turned her head toward Grandad saying "You know I HATE that picture. Mother made me wear that contraption and I looked cheap."

The good news was that after that, the silence was broken... but only for the kids. She had moved Grandad into the guest room. She told the kids she would feed and clothe him... but that's it. It wasn't until February 14th that she spoke to him again.

There was a Valentine's Potluck after Church. Grandad had made sure the kids stayed behind so he could give Grandmother her Valentines Gift. Grandad ran home during Bible class to set up her surprise.

Finally, when they pulled into the driveway, he said "You know, you are the love of my life." While getting out of the car, she matter-of-factly replied "OK."

Slowly they walked up the sidewalk. Trying to take her hand, she pulled away. Grandad rushed in front of her and opened the front door. There, sitting on the entry table was a long silver box. She smiled.

She slid the red ribbon off the box, opening to find a dozen, long-stemmed roses.

Her smile disappeared. Her eyes started tearing up. She looked at him and whispered, "Red roses are YOUR favorite flower, not mine".

Grandad stood still.

She closed the box and headed into the kitchen. Grandad followed behind. She swung the door open... and gasped. Every corner, every inch of that kitchen was covered with seventeen dozen yellow roses.

"Every yellow rose from Oklahoma, New Mexico, and Texas they could find... just for you... and the seventeen years I've known you."

Taking her hand and looking into her eyes, Grandad continued, "I know... yellow is your favorite color. You love it because it reminds you of summer", pausing, his voice cracked "and happiness".

Grandmother couldn't stop crying.


On Friday, December 17, 1954, my Aunt Robin was born.

# THE SHOCK OF FAILURE

From school to the Hospital, Sharri couldn't stop... and couldn't stop her tears.

It felt like rivers of every emotion flowing down her face. She knew her mascara would be on her white School T-shirt. She couldn't even call her husband Steve...

"WHY?" Sharri screamed.

As the road curved through the thicket around Liberty, Sharri kept thinking about how her Mom raised her. On her own, after her Dad walked out, she kept everything together. She fed, clothed, provided Thanksgiving, Christmas, birthdays, boyfriend guidance... everything... on a miserly Teaching salary, and basically all alone.

When Dad casually walked back into her life three weeks before High School Graduation, Sherri's anger was beyond boiling. Her Mom, always gracious, always kind, never spoke a harsh word regarding her Father. She even defended him by telling her to allow him to be a part of her life.

Like always, Sharri's Dad disappeared from her life until each of life's next big events.

"Just in time for pictures.", she would tell Steve sarcastically.

Sharri's Mom had been there for every birthday party for her girls. She paid for her college and her wedding. She helped her move to New York, then to LA, and then back to Texas. And then, when the pandemic happened, and Steve lost his job, they needed a roof over their heads. What did she do? Understanding their financial strain, she insisted they move home to live with her to get back on their feet. Then Steve got the job in Dayton, and now they were just 20 minutes away.

'We just got here. We just got here.' Sharri kept thinking with defeat.

Sherri began to pull into Liberty/Dayton Medical Center. Taking a big, deep breath to collect her thoughts and emotions, she saw her husband's car next to her Mom's car. She was so relieved to know that Steve was there and could assess how bad her Mom was.

Running toward the front doors, the drizzle had made the cement slick, and it almost made Sharri trip. However, she caught herself from completely face-planting and making matters much, much worse.

The doors of the tiny Hospital slid open as she rushed into the arms of her awaiting husband. As she stood there sobbing in his chest, she mumbled the question "Is she going to survive?".

That's when Sharri heard her Mom's voice. "Sweetie."

Sharri looked up with disbelief.

What was going on here? Why was Mom standing here in the entry of the Hospital with Steve?

Milly looked directly at Sharri and said, "Sweetie, it's your Dad. He's not going to survive the afternoon."

All tears were replaced with sheer anger. "WHY DID YOU DRAG ME AWAY FROM SCHOOL FOR THIS?"

Steve answered her... Mrs. Shannon, from your Mom's church, pretended to be the nurse. We all knew you needed to say goodbye to him.

"WHAT?" Sharri yelled...

Steve continued, "We knew you wouldn't come unless you thought it was your Mom."

"THAT MAN HAS MANIPULATED ME ONE TOO MANY TIMES.  ENOUGH IS ENOUGH!"

Milly raised her voice for the first time in 30 years.

"Now LISTEN Sharri. That's ENOUGH. Now get your butt in there. At least say goodbye...", then yelling, "NOW!"

Sharri had never disobeyed her Mother. So, like the rule follower she had always been, she slowly started following the Nurse.

Milly walked with her and told Sharri to brace herself. Milly took her hand. That's when Sharri turned to her and asked, "Why are you always protecting him?  He walked out of our lives. He was there only when it was convenient for HIM."

Milly began tearing up. "He showed up sober for YOU. He couldn't ever do it for himself, not even for me. But for you... He showed up for YOU."

Sharri stopped in the center of the hallway. With her voice cracking, she said "He never smelled like alcohol."

Milly continued, "He would start drying out for three days before he was supposed to see you. That's why he always shook so much."

Both were silent. Sharri couldn't move. Everything was different. Now, like being hit by a two-by-four in the face, she remembered every time he showed up for her. Everything changed. Everything changed in that moment.

Milly continued, "I have been telling you for months and months that you need to go see him. Steve's been coming by and bringing the girls. When he started changing colors, he had to stop bringing them."

That's when Sharri realized that her girls have known all along. They had a deeper connection with her own Father because Steve helped them understand.

"You're the only one who refused to see him."

Sharri suddenly felt beyond any guilt she had ever felt in her life. That's when Milly said, "Run to him."

And Sharri did.

# T-Tops

It's September.

In typical 80's form, JT's hair had begun turning from bleached blonde into a brownish floppy bob. Always in board shorts, an Ocean Pacific T-shirt and shiny white K-Swiss tennis shoes, he looked ready for any beach. Unfortunately for JT, the closest beach was more than seven hours away. At least he could dream about the beach, or dream about the girls who never talked to him.

JT was always daydreaming. Once again, daydreaming had gotten him into trouble. This time, he was grounded from his car for two weeks, and today was Debate Club.

The team always prepared for competition after school. Last Thursday, they collectively decided to meet at the school library, split up and then head out to the college for better research. So, when JT arrived late as usual, he knew he had to hitch a ride with someone.

Unfortunately, the only person remaining was Jennifer. Now, there's nothing wrong with Jennifer; she's a cute, sweet girl. However, JT could feel how much she liked him. They had been in almost every class and competition together most of their lives.

However today, JT did a double take. Jennifer usually had her hair pulled back into a ponytail. And she seemed to always be staring at him. But today, her hair was down; she didn't even look like the 'normal' Jennifer. After a little chit-chat, she suggested he drive her car. Of course, JT agreed.

As they walked together toward the outside door, she told JT that her dad had given her birthday present a week early. At that moment, she opened the door and there sat a black Buick Riviera with T-Tops. It had black leather interior, black mag wheels, and a spoiler.

JT gasped and screamed "SCHWEET"! Just the sight of that gleaming sports coupe made JT giddy. Jennifer then threw him the keys and said, "let's go".

They hopped in, and slowly started their drive out to the College. Jennifer asked him why he was driving so slowly? JT was a little nervous to be driving such an awesome car. His mind kept racing, questioning what if he damaged it or even wrecked it? His parents would kill him. Finally, JT spoke.

Stammering he said, "I'm a little scared of..."

Just as JT was about to finish his comment, Jennifer used both her hands to push his leg down, gunning the accelerator. Much to both of their surprise, it worked. That car kicked into a passing gear. The motor revved loudly, launching it into some sort of sports car stratospheric ascent.

After three blocks of exhilaration, they slowed to a stop at the corner they were supposed to turn to head to the College. Jennifer leaned over again, turning JT's head toward her. Staring directly into his eyes, Jennifer said with a sinister grin, "let's take it for a spin... we won't be long."

JT's mind contemplated what all could go wrong. But, when JT's mouth opened, he heard himself say "OK". And forward the two went.

After twenty minutes, the two finally made it to the College Library. As they pulled into the parking lot, Jennifer thanked him. A puzzled JT asked why she was thanking him.

"For my first kiss" ... JT abruptly turned to look over at her, only to have his lips meet hers.

And just like that, Jennifer had her first kiss... and so did JT.

# WHEN GRAN WAS YOUNG

Since the age of three, Fitz would practice on that old piano back in Gran's converted garage Art Studio. He had studied every inch of that Studio. Through elementary and part of junior high, he would go to Gran's to practice every day. Each day he would bounce across the deck, then down the steps, and run back out to Gran's 'abandoned' Garage studio.

In the ninth grade, Fitz broke his leg. Like each day after school, he stayed with Gran. Normally, this wouldn't have been a problem; however, with a broken leg, crutches, and a backpack, the navigation to the back studio, up, down, and around each obstacle became quite treacherous. All he wanted to do was to catch a breath. Sweat poured out of every pore in his body. By the time he could finally plop in that great, big, fluffy chair, he was afraid his sweat would further stain the faded pink paisley.

As he sank into Gran's cozy seat, he looked up. On the top shelf of the tallest bookcase in that studio, sat a small wood box with a large feather painted on the outside. On April 14, 1994, and for the 'bazillionth' time, his curiosity got to him again, asking Gran what was in that box. For years, she had diverted her grandson's curiosity and wonder. But on that day, she sighed saying, "Well, I guess you're ready. I'll be right back with some goodies". Jokingly, Fitz said "Need some help?"

Gran was spry for her 78 years. She was quite proud of walking the 'bowels around Hell' which is how she referred to the neighborhood surrounding her old house. That day, she returned with a tray of lemonade and every sugar cookie in the house, knowing that this day would forever change their relationship.

She took deep breaths the entire way to and from the House. She had been preparing herself for this day. She wanted to tell him when she felt the time was right. She would think,

'Fourteen years old... that's old enough'. She just knew he'd be able to grasp and understand the contents inside that box. His Mother never had any interest regarding her past.

After she gave him some cookies and lemonade, Gran pulled up her beat up, tufted floor cushion. With a deep breath, she began. She started talking about New York and her pipe dreams. She suddenly realized she had forgotten the box. So, up she went, grabbing that stupid box off the top shelf. It's almost like she never took a breath. She just kept talking about her childhood, dreams of becoming a famous artist... or maybe even a dancer. But she knew, it wasn't going to happen down here.

When she was sixteen, in the middle of the Great Depression, she was only two years older than Fitz. Against her Mother's wishes, she decided to run away to New York. She believed the City would inspire her art. Her Dad had a soft spot for her. Being a moderately wealthy oilman, he not only gave her permission, but gave her an expense account.

Looking back on her life, she could now admit that she didn't have any real concept of money. She was considered a free spirit. She was an artist, not a realist. She explained to Fitz that she had so many regrets. She said that even in her youth, her carefree ideas would make the 1960's look 'pure' and 'drama-free'. She wanted to explore! The world was a big place, and she believed in absolute, unconditional, free love.

The minute she said, 'free love', Fitz's mouth dropped. Slowly and emphasizing the word free, he questioned, "What do you mean by FREE love"?

There was a long pause. Gran answered by saying, "It's an expression. Like 'Love doesn't cost anything, except your heart'. So, don't just give your love to anyone. Love matters."

"What are you talking about?" Fitz asked.

Gran stood up, twirled around and then popped a pose, like some 'Broadway Star'. "I wanted to paint... and dance... and have sex, and have new experiences, and..." Fitz interrupted... "SEX?"

She plopped back down on that big cushion again. "Yes. Your Gran was promiscuous. I did not discriminate."

Fitz' eyes were bigger than silver dollar coins. "Why are you telling me this?"

Sheepishly, she looked at him and said, "Your Gran understands. I want you to be you."

Fitz looked puzzled, "You want me to have sex? UUUUUUH."

With exasperation, she said, "Uh, NO... no, no, no. That's not what I'm saying. You need to follow your heart. I'm talking about your music."

At that moment, Gran opened the box and dumped about twenty paper fliers in his lap. They were hand drawn, painted, and had a 1935 date on them. But what caught his eye was her name across the top.

"YOU HAD AN ART SHOW!!!! I thought you said..." Fitz tried to leap out of his seat, but couldn't because of that stupid cast, and being too deep in the chair.

She interrupted, "No. That's the point. I planned an Art Show. I planned, and planned, and planned. I had a venue, had interested Gallery owners... dealers... and then I met Adolfo."

"Wait... who?" Fitz looked a little concerned.

"Your Mom's biological Father... your Grandfather. Your Mom has never wanted to know about him or any of this."

"Whaaaat?" Fitz questioned.

"Let me explain", so she described New York life. How she loved the city, the pace, the atmosphere, the movement, the inspiration, the music, the dancing... on and on she continued until she said "Adolfo".

Her silence and contemplative look spoke volumes. With a tired whisper, she said, "Everything changed… Everything."

"I was set to hit it big. My gut knew it… in fact everyone knew it. All of my friends, my Dad… even my Mom knew it. But Adolfo wanted me to go to Paris with him. It was that week. THAT week, and of all weeks. My friends tried to talk me out of it. He was supposed to perform at the opera. He said he needed my support. He couldn't play without me…" With a tone of disdain, and while rolling her eyes she finished, "or so he claimed."

Fitz looked angry. Adamantly he stated, "You are always telling me to follow my dreams." And in a hokey, pompous voice, Fitz continued, "Don't let anyone, or anything come between you and your music."

Fitz was so mad. He couldn't even look at his Gran.

Bluntly, she said, "I told you that so you wouldn't have regrets… like I did. Don't get me wrong, I will never regret your Mom. But it's the timing I regret… and, if I wouldn't have gone to Paris, I wouldn't have your Mom… and I wouldn't have you."

After a brief silence, she said "and Adolfo was a fabulous pianist… just like you. In fact …"

Pausing for a moment, she got up again. She walked over to the bookcase and pulled out a small envelope. Inside there was a small picture. Staring back at Fitz was the face of a young man in his twenties… who happened to look exactly like Fitz.

"Look at him. Just look at him." Gran said sternly.

"Every time I look at you, I see him. Every time I talk to you… he's alive again. I see him in you. Look at him. The way you look… the way you play… your passion, HIS passion. His and your fever pitches are inside of your playing. It's like…"

Trailing off, her voice weakened saying "Your Mom could never understand. As an Artist I never had this/that with your mom. She looks like me, and she acts like my mother. She's too logical for art. And when you sat down at Adolfo's piano and started playing... I almost passed out."

Fitz was startled, "That's Adolfo's piano?"

"Yes. It WAS Adolfo's piano. It's the only thing that survived the fire. We shipped it back here after he..."

Fitz didn't know how to react. He just sat there. Then he mustered just enough gumption to ask, "So he's dead?"

"Yes..." Gran paused. Choking up, Gran tried to compose herself. "Well, I did swear I would tell you." Suddenly, Gran started to panic. Her breathing became short and heavy. Then, she just began sobbing uncontrollably. She buried her face in her hands, mumbling, "I can't believe this, I'm falling apart... right now... after all these years... why right now?"

Fitz sat stunned. He'd never seen his Gran so vulnerable. She was always so composed, so full of passion and drive. This was something new. This was different. Something deep from within her was erupting. This was from some unknown place. Somehow, Fitz understood. He just knew and understood in his soul.

Slowly, Fitz maneuvered out of the chair. Sliding over and sitting in front of Adolfo's piano and began playing.

Gran sighed. There were no more tears. She just sat staring, mesmerized by her beautiful grandson. Music filled the garage's musty air as Fitz, Adolfo Fitzsimmons Waughkufka played Chopin's Nocturne No. 2 in E-Flat Major.

Scooting over to that old chair, Gran sank deep, disappearing inside that paisley pink fabric. Looking up, she noticed that the sun was setting. Crossing her arms and leaning back, she propped her feet upon the floor cushion. She sat listening and smiling, watching the dust glisten from the sun rays peeping through those old garage door windows.

# THE LONG RIDE HOME

The seventeen-minute drive into town, usually wasn't a long drive.

Derrick and Stephen had just left their entire family at the Barn. Mama told the boys to drive into town and get more ice. Normally, she'd just do it herself, but this was a special occasion. She and Big Daddy were too busy with the wedding and couldn't leave.

Neither Derrick nor Stephen could fathom WHY on Earth their sister would choose to get married in a Barn, especially in the summertime... in Texas... with the day's high being 105. That Barn had no fans, no misters, no 'swamp' coolers... nothing to cool the dry, Texas air. So as everyone sat there on bales of hay, sweat poured out of every section of their bodies. Their Mother must have been crazy to approve sitting on bales of hay for a wedding, especially in the summertime.

Well, she was her only girl. Her sister Pat's only daughter, whom she raised after Pat died of cancer. But to the brothers, this whole fiasco was just plain, ole, lunacy. Why not wait until Fall. And now their Mama was sending the brothers out to get more ice.

"I bet this is the hottest wedding ever". Stephen waited on Derrick's response, knowing that he must have been thinking the exact same thing. Continuing, he said "Even Kitty is sweating!"

Derrick replied in his usual sheepish tone, "Mom seems to be holding it together pretty good." He was wondering how their Mother could be so positive about marrying off Kitty. They've called Kathryn, 'Kitty' forever! Aunt Pat's pride and joy was 'cute as a kitten', so 'Kitty' stuck.

Kitty beauty was breath-taking. But having brothers, brought her down to Earth. Since they were around the same age, they grew up with a special bond. That was, until Kitty met Biker Dude.

Biker Dude's real name was Sean. 'Sean' referred to himself in third person, which immensely irritated Derrick. And 'Sean' was a political science major. And 'Sean' was planning on becoming a lawyer. And 'Sean' rode a Harley. They figured the 'bad-boy, danger' factor is what attracted Kitty to Biker Dude.

Those boys had always been overprotective of Kitty. Afterall, who better to protect a sister than her brothers. The three of them were extremely close. Stephen was only a couple of months older than Kitty, and Derrick was born nine months after her. She had been through so much in her life. Especially after her mom died, and their parents formally adopted Kathryn.

So, as Stephen and Derrick were driving into town to get ice for Kitty's wedding, it was inevitable that the brothers would go down memory lane. They started talking and laughing about all of the different family vacations and adventures. Of course, the beginning of the conversation was the obvious topic of air-conditioning. Nothing could feel better than the air-conditioner in Stephen's car, a 1977 Orange Pontiac Firebird. Stephen had given it the nickname 'Big Bird'.

The night was pitch dark out in the country. As they sped through each curve, the blackness behind them made the red taillights illuminate the flying dirt. Stephen was a crazy driver. Derrick was holding onto the door handle for his life.

Just as the boys were taking one of the final curves, and just after the largest thicket of mesquite trees, their headlights suddenly hit two white, glowing dots in the middle of the road. Those white dots where the eyes of a deer. Derrick screamed

"DEER", as Stephen slammed on the brakes. The car started skidding as Stephen screamed back at Derrick.

To miss the deer, Stephen turned 'Big Bird' to the left as quickly as possible. 'Big Bird' started spinning out of control. From doing donuts out in the pastures, whether through sand or snow, Stephen had learned to turn into the spin.

Finally, the car stopped. 'Big Bird' was in the middle of the dirt road facing the opposite direction. Both boys sighed. Relief and silence swallowed the car.

The boys couldn't catch their breath. Finally, Stephen spoke.

"Luckily, 'Big Bird' was unphased and held his ground..."

After a long pause, "DERRICK... are you listening to me?"

Meekly, "yes... 'Big Bird' held its ground. Stephen..." Derrick stammered "I have to tell you something."

"WHAT."

Derrick was facing the window when he spoke. "I was talking to Kitty today... and she said, well... she said I should talk to you, too. SO, do you think you'll ever get married? You know, like Kitty?"

"Uhhhhh... yeah. Hopefully to Jennifer... well if she wants too. Why?"

Derrick swallowed hard, voice cracking as he started speaking again. "I don't know. I just don't know... well, that's not true. I do know. I DO know. Ya know?"

"HUH? What are you talking about? You're not making sense." Stephen was getting confused and irritated by this line of conversation. "Is it the deer? 'Cause, you know it's ok! We're ok, and the deer's ok. We didn't kill an animal. Don't be such a titty-baby."

"NOOOO. I'm not a baby. It's, it's me. I want to get married too" as Derrick's voice trailed off, "just not to Jennifer."

"Of course not. She's mine... not yours." Stephen started getting angry and became even more confused. He knew that Derrick was trying to put something into words. "DAMN-IT DERRICK... Just blurt it out. Whatever you need to say, just say it. And you'll feel better."

"It's when Sean kissed Kitty. Could you see yourself kissing up there?"

"EWWWW, Kitty's my sister! She's OUR sister. That's gross. What's wrong with you?"

"NO. It's not about kissing Kitty... it's about Sean." Derrick started breathing heavier.

Stephen just sat there in the silence.

"It's like when I saw her kissing Sean, well, before... I knew..."

Stephen yelled at Derrick "OH MY GAWD... YOU'RE A FAGGOT?"

Derrick turned to Stephen with tears rolling down his face. "I'm not a fag. I just... oh never mind."

"What then? You said you wanted to kiss Sean? You said you didn't want to kiss her, so what is it? It can't be both."

Derrick stammered saying, "I said, NEVERMIND!" Derrick turned back to the window. Trying to keep his emotions together, he could see his own tears rolling down his cheeks from the light reflected by the dashboard.

Stephen grunted and yelled "WHATEVER". Slamming his foot to the accelerator, he just started driving again. The rest of the way into town, and back to the barn, neither one spoke another word.

After Stephen parked in front of the barn, he turned to Derrick. "You know it's wrong. God hates fags. You know it's wrong, and God hates you for it."

And just like that, Stephen got out of the car and grabbed two of the bags of ice. Then, barking orders, he told Derrick to get the rest of the bags to 'make a man out of him'.

The rest of the evening went off without a hitch. Mama told her other sisters that the only problem she could assess was the heat and running out of ice. So overall, she was so very pleased with how everything turned out.

By the end of the evening, the air had cooled, and everyone was laughing and smiling as Sean and Kitty left. Down the dirt road they drove, ready to start their new lives together.

By this time, it was almost one am. Everyone in the whole family had pitched in to help tear down and clean up. Mama asked Stephen where Derrick had disappeared. With a snarky tone, Stephen said he was probably hiding to get out of work. Then he told her he wasn't his brother's keeper and called him a fag. That's when his Mother slapped him.

Big Daddy saw what Mama did and walked over. He asked Stephen what he said to make her so angry. After he heard what he said, he told Stephen to go find Derrick. Stephen was about to talk back when he saw that look in Big Daddy's eyes. He knew he'd better just suck it up and go find the 'fag'.

After twenty minutes, Stephen came back with a look of disdain, and a tone of disregard. "I can't find him anywhere. I guess he hid well."

It had been nine years since Sean and Kathryn had married. Her oldest boy entered the kitchen after being outside with all the cousins. DJ had a bloody nose... again.

"What happened this time?"

"Mom. Uncle Stephen hit me with the football... again. He said I need to man-up."

Kathryn went to the door and yelled at Stephen. "Stephen, REALLY? You could have at least told him to tilt his head back and hold his nose. And he needs to MAN-UP? What MAN doesn't tell a kid how to fix a bloody nose? I have warned you for the last time... MR. MAN!" Kathryn threw her hands in the air and turned around.

Stephen rolled his eyes, looked at his son and said, "I'm telling you again! You're not a wimp like DJ. And especially don't be like your Uncle Derrick... that fag'll rot in Hell."

When Kathryn heard Stephen's words, her anger burned far hotter than any hell he could imagine. Storming back into the house, she slammed the back door shut. Turning to Sean, she said, "That's it. THAT IS IT. THAT is the last time he will ever be welcomed in our home. He has no regard for anyone... or anything. I'm DONE with him."

As Kathryn burst into tears, she rushed out of the kitchen and up the stairs. Lowering his head back down while still holding his nose, DJ spoke up, "Dad, why does Mom always start crying when Uncle Stephen talks bad about me and Uncle Derrick?"

"DJ, your Uncle Derrick was gay. He probably thinks you are too. Your Uncle Derrick had just told your Mom before he hung himself on our wedding night. She still blames herself leaving and for telling him to tell Stephen."

With a look of concern DJ asked "But... why would he kill himself?"

Sean looked down, then back up at his son. Fighting tears, he replied, "I guess" ...

Then after a long pause he continued, "I guess, he just didn't feel like anyone cared or loved him."

# LIONEL GATES FINAL BOW

"Twas the night before Christmas"... Lionel's booming voice cracked, but he faithfully continued tradition.

He had recited the most famous Christmas poem every year for the past 53 years. At 5:30pm every Christmas Eve, everyone in their small town gathered at the City Auditorium. It was the 'Annual Christmas Spectacular'. Somehow, he'd let his best friend talk him into reciting that stupid poem 53 years ago.

For that first event, Margaret, whom everyone called Peggy, decided her 'Lionel Gates' needed to dress 'festive' for his performance. She made him a simple vest using Christmas Plaid fabric with ornate gold buttons. Along with the vest, he wore a simple white oxford shirt, black slacks, red socks, and penny loafers. It wasn't much to look at, but he wore that exact same combination for the next twelve years. In everyone's minds, this had become a new Christmas tradition.

Year thirteen was hard. Peggy had finally succumbed to her cancer in April. Come November, the Christmas Council begged, and begged Lionel to go ahead and recite the poem. After much thought, Lionel finally agreed. The day before the performance, Christmas Eve's Eve, he put on his usual attire. The problem with it this time was the shirt was way too big, and his slacks couldn't stay up. In the last year, he'd lost so much weight, he couldn't even belt his pants up to make them look better.

Lionel realized it was time for him to update his outfit. So, mustering up an ounce of courage, he marched downtown to different shops searching for some new clothes. To this day, he still doesn't know why, but he wandered into Miss Hattie's Personality Shop. That's where and when he met the beautiful, funny Hadley, Miss Hattie's daughter. She'd just moved back to take over her Mom's shop. Hadley told Lionel that he looked like he needed some help.

Grabbing that tattered vest from Lionel's hands, she looked directly into Lionel's eyes and stated loudly, "Mom, take over for me. Lionel needs my help for the Christmas Spectacular." And off they went.

Two hours later, Lionel had a brand new, thick red oxford, navy chinos, and new socks with a Christmas tree print. Hadley told Lionel that she needed the evening to work on that old vest. Being a master seamstress, she told Lionel to brace himself. She would have that vest refurbished in Peggy's honor. Then, she told him that he could pick it up at her house tomorrow at Noon, and she'd cook him some lunch.

All night Lionel thought about Hadley. Lunch couldn't get here fast enough, but it did. And as Lionel walked up to the house, approaching the porch, he could smell the fried chicken. When he rang the bell, Hadley yelled to just come on in because it was open. He walked in slowly and there, lying on a seafoam green sofa was a shirt box. Lionel walked over to it, lifted the lid, and pulled back the tissue.

Inside was that tattered vest, transformed into something old world. It was now trimmed with dark green suede, gold cord, and crushed burgundy velvet. She had even lined the vest with red satin. Lionel teared up thinking how Peggy would have loved it. She loved everything about Christmas. That's when he heard Hadley say, "I love Christmas, don't you? Sorry I have so many Santa's. My Grandmother collected them, and I inherited them... and I just seem to keep adding more."

Lionel looked up. He hadn't noticed that he was surrounded by over 200 Santa's. Every size and shape imaginable sat on every table and shelf. Lionel started laughing, following with, "If you need about 70 more, I have some for you." Now snickering he said, "I collect them too."

The vest fit perfect, and the meal was wonderful; and Lionel didn't even want to leave Hadley's home. He knew he had already fallen in love with Hadley.

That evening, the Christmas Spectacular went off without a hitch, and was a big hit. So was Lionel's new vest. Everyone noticed how happy Lionel seemed. But more importantly, they noticed how he was looking at Hadley.

Two days after the year anniversary of Peggy's death, Hadley and Lionel were married down at the United Methodist Church.

After two sons, two daughters, husbands, wives, and eleven grandkids, Lionel and Hadley were ecstatic. They hadn't told anyone in the community that they had sold their house to their grandson. Lionel had retired from the Post Office, and Hadley had just sold the Shop to their grandson's wife. Lionel and Hadley were living out their dream and moving to Santa Fe.

Lionel was almost finished reciting the poem. That's when he froze.

Lionel just stopped. He just stopped. The entire audience took a breath. Lionel looked out at the audience, then over to Hadley who was smiling brightly with joy. Then, he looked down. He could see his tears hitting the wood stage. He couldn't control himself. That's when he felt a hand on his right hand... it was Jack, his grandson, beaming from ear to ear. He realized at that moment, that Jack was wearing a new red oxford, navy chinos, red Christmas socks, and penny loafers.

Lionel slightly stepped back, slipped off his vest and slid it onto Jack. Brushing the wrinkles off his back, Lionel looked on with more pride than anyone could imagine. Jack picked up right where he had left off. He was about to finish when he turned to his grandad and said "Papaw, why don't you close us out".

Looking at his grandson, then looking back at the audience, he said in his deep, booming, voice, "Happy Christmas to all, and to all a good night."

Together, they bowed.

Hmmm... is that it?  I guess so.

Made in the USA
Coppell, TX
08 April 2022

76198498R10051